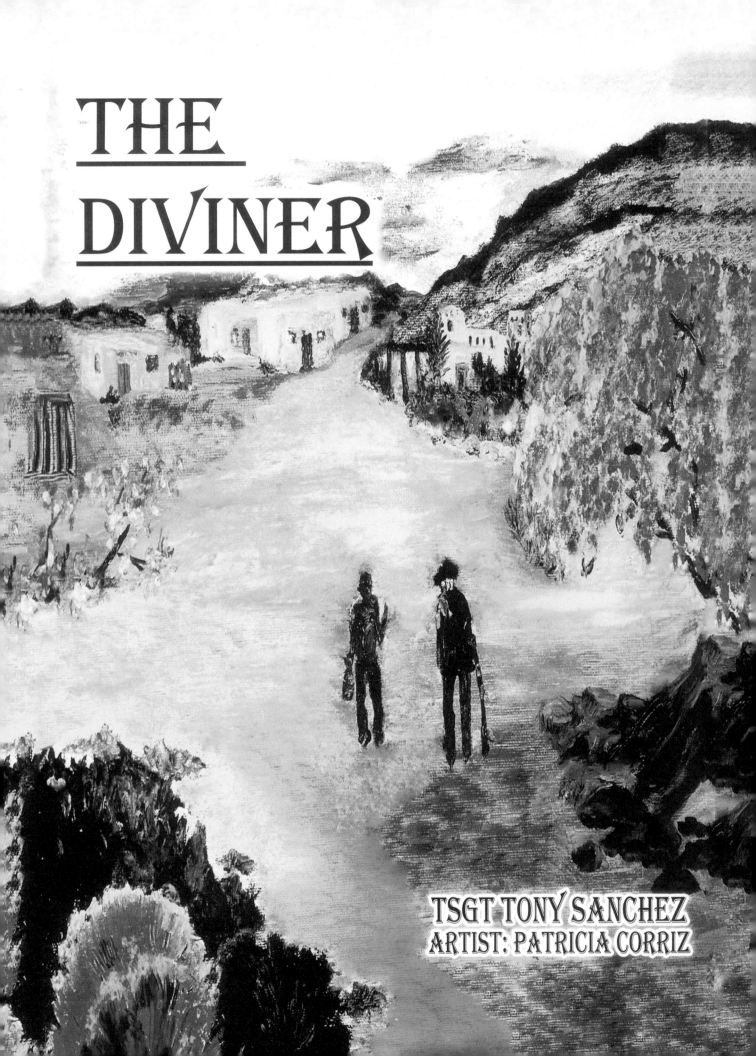

THE
DIVINER

TSGT TONY SANCHEZ
ARTIST: PATRICIA CORRIZ

THE DIVINER

iUniverse books may be ordered through booksellers or by contacting:

iUniverse
1663 Liberty Drive
Bloomington, IN 47403
www.iuniverse.com
1-800-Authors (1-800-288-4677)

Because of the dynamic nature of the Internet, any web addresses or links contained in this book may have changed since publication and may no longer be valid. The views expressed in this work are solely those of the author and do not necessarily reflect the views of the publisher, and the publisher hereby disclaims any responsibility for them.

Any people depicted in stock imagery provided by Getty Images are models,
and such images are being used for illustrative purposes only.
Certain stock imagery © Getty Images.

ISBN: 978-1-5320-5894-3 (sc)
ISBN: 978-1-5320-5895-0 (e)

Library of Congress Control Number: 2018912593

Print information available on the last page.

iUniverse rev. date: 12/13/2018

DEDICATION

I dedicate this book to Susan who always encouraged me whenever I needed it most.

The Turquoise Rose
of New Mexico

Tsgt Tony Sanchez

El Santuario de Chimayo

"Tis a land of faith this mountain land
Where God has come to bless mankind
This old Spanish church built so long ago
Along silent streams where great rivers flow
Where old worn out crutches rest upon its ancient walls
A testament of miracles that have come to be
Resting there in silence for all to see
Where purple mountains breathe a quiet sigh
Leaving those of us to wonder and ponder "why"
Oh! Holy little church our faith renew
Making us as children where all is new
Knowing that the love of God is there for all to see
Praying in this little church kneeling in humility
Going on forever until the end of time
Knowing the deep love of God for all mankind
Oh holy little chapel
God has smiled upon thee

Tsgt Tony Sanchez

The Diviner

by

TSgt Tony Sanchez

This is the story of Miguel de Otero, a man who loved life and lived it as completely as God intended it to be.

The Lord said to Moses..."Take your shepherd's Staff and strike the rock and water will come pouring out"... And so it did... The Book of Exodus Chapter 17, Versus 5-6.

The bright orange sun was rising out of the east. It was showing off its brilliant purple and orange light. The sun's warm yellow rays of golden sunlight were just starting to dance off the early morning turquoise mist. It was the deepest part of the Terento Valley, high in the Sangra de Cristo Mountains. There were thick stands of tall dark green Colorado Pines. There was also fragrant Northern New Mexico light bluish Pinion Trees. It was here that the young boy stood.

He was tall and thin for his years. The boy's skin was the color of dry roasted pinions. His hair was light brown and his eyes sky blue. His eyes were now set with a strong look of determination. The boy was standing over an old man who was resting on the ground. Moving his hands under the old man's arms, he lifted him up helping him back to his feet.

They were standing just below the snow line as the bright golden orange rays of light reflected off the white fluffy snow. The bright light was causing the boy to shade his eyes. He was staring up the side of the mountain to where the old man was pointing at.

"Alli' esta!" "It is there! That is where we must go!" he cried out. The old man was pointing to a small ledge of dark blue iron ore that was protruding half way up the side of the mountain.

"But that is very high Don Arturo; can you climb that far?" the boy asked.

"Si...Miguel, I must, for that is where I have come to die!" he said, his eyes were sad as he contemplated his own death. Helping the old man, Miguel half pushed and half carried him up the side of the mountain.

While resting on a ledge Miguel could see a small opening. It appeared large enough for a person to crawl through. The sides of the mountain were light colored granite, inter-faced with shades of crimson and turquoise colored rock.

Walking forward his feet kept slipping on loose purple and red colored stones that made for a narrow foot path. Pulling the old man through the opening while the sun was at midday, its light bluish rays of sunlight were making the boy sweat. Reaching for the bottle of water that he carried in the gunny sack, he drank deeply quenching his great thirst. Wiping off his forehead, he followed the old man into the narrow cave

The entrance led to a dark cavern, where the boy allowed his eyes to get accustomed to the grayish light. Looking at the loose gravel he saw where the old man had gone. Following the footsteps he came to a narrow passageway where bright golden sunshine was streaming through. Walking further he came to a large chamber where the old man sat. He was sitting at a large table and appeared to be holding an oversized ledger. The old man's face was now bathed in dark grayish light and appeared to be at peace with himself. When he saw the boy he motioned him over pointing to a seat next to him.

"Be seated Miguel, for I have much to show you with the little time I have left, " he said, a slight smile forming at the corners of his mouth. "I was about your age when I first came to this place. It was Don Francisco de Ortega who brought me here. He was the Diviner for San Geronimo at the time. "Look there" he said, pointing to a spot on the ledger.

"That is where he made his mark. He could neither read nor write, yet he was one of the wisest men I ever knew. "Mira aqui", look here at the date, what does it say?"

"It says 17 August in the year of our Lord 1875 and it shows the mark that Don Francisco made. There! I see your name written too, ''Demetrius Juan Arturo'', and where you signed and dated it, but what is this place?" asked the boy.

The chamber that he and the old man were in was made up of one large room that was almost fifty feet wide and some two hundred yards long. As Miguel stood up and walked around, he took in everything that was around him. There on the far wall was a Spanish Coat of Arms. Next to it was a helmet and bronze chest plate with three lances stacked neatly next to it. On the wall behind where Don Arturo sat, was a sheet of white granite that ran some twenty feet up the side of the cave. There must have been some artisans in the group, for the wall was covered with paintings depicting various events of exploration and later colonization of the new world.

"This is quite a wonder," Miguel said, as he walked staring in disbelief.

"Yes, but now we must do what we came for," Don Arturo said. "I feel that soon I will be joining the others whose names are written in the book. I have already signed it, now all you have to do is put your name next to mine then sign it." Moving to the ancient scroll the boy printed his full Christian name ''Miguel Antonio de Otero'' then he signed it.

"There, that is done, and now we must go outside. There is much to show you with so little time Don Arturo said, with most of the color draining from his face. "Come this way," he said standing up with Miguel helping him along.-

Walking slowly, he turned to the north side of the cave where there appeared to be another entrance, only much larger than the first one. As he moved closer, Miguel saw that it led out. Walking further he heard the sound of water as it fell to the ground. Moving through the entrance, the bright purplish sun seemed to be at midday. Looking toward the sound of the cascading water, he stared at the waterfall, its dark blue water flowing down the mountain side.

Off to the side, the boy saw a large pool of light green colored water surrounded by reddish brown rock. It was here that the light green water gathered forming into the largest of the pools. At the base of the pool, stood one of the largest weeping willows trees the boy had ever seen. It was over 200 feet tall with its long branches hanging over most of the pool.

"There, that is where we must go!" the old man cried, "It is there that you must dig my grave," he said walking with the boy to the base of the tree.

"But why here, Don Arturo?" he asked setting the gunny sack down. "Because, this is where I must end my days," he whispered as the spark of life slowly drained from his eyes.

"What is this place?"

"It is where you must journey back each year," the old man said looking at the willow tree. "You will cut one of its branches here where it forks," he said, pulling down one of the branches. "See, how this one formed with a perfect V! It is one like this that you must measure and cut. Then you cut off the branch exactly five feet from the trunk. Inside is a measuring stick that is five feet long. You must use it every time. Once the branch is cut and you offer it up to the four winds with the sacred prayer, which I will speak to you about, then you will be the new Diviner of San Geronimo.

"Yes I understand," the boy said, not exactly sure that he did, but hoping that he would.

"When you come back it must be in the springtime when the bright yellow sunflowers are just starting to bloom. It will be when herds of elk and mule deer will be coming back to the high meadows to graze. Then too, the wild geese will fill the sky by the thousands with their bright feathered bodies and their black feathered wing tips. Also great flocks of great northern ducks, their deep dark green heads and light yellow beaks will also fill the sky as they began their long journey back to the North Country."

The boy wondered if he would remember any of this. He knew that he must as he looked at the old man who had begun to speak again. "Now listen to my words carefully" he whispered as he fought to draw his last breath. "You must always come alone, the only time you will bring someone else is when you are old and feel that your days are few. That is when you will bring the one that you have chosen and trained to be the next Diviner of San Geronimo. You will teach him of this place just as I have taught you. He too, will sign his name to the ancient scroll, then he will bury you just as you are about to do to me. These are the words that you must say to the four winds he whispered with his last breath. "Oh four winds, come to San Geronimo when you are needed; bring rain and snow and sunshine in their time. Let the "acequias" be filled with life giving water in your holy name Lord...Amen."

"I understand Don Arturo," the boy said, holding the old man's head in his lap as his life slowly drifted from his eyes. Remembering "Las Mañanitas" was his favorite song, the boy began singing it slowly... "Estas son las mañanitas que cantaba el "Rey David."

This is the morning song that King David sang.

"Hoy por ser dia de tu santo, te las cantamos a ti." "Because today is your saint's day we're singing it for you"

"Despierta mi bien despierta,mira que ya amanecio." "Wake up, wake up, look it's already dawn."

"Ya los pajarillos cantan,la luna ya se metio." "The birds are already singing and the moon has set."

"Que'linda esta' la mañana en que vengo a saludarte. Venimos todos con gusto y placer a felicitarte." "How lovely is the morning in which I come to greet you? We all come with joy and pleasure to congratulate you."

"Ya viene amaneciendo, ya la luz del dia' nos dio." "The morning is coming now, the sun is giving us its light."

"Leva'ntate de mañ'ana, mira que ya amanecio." "Get up in the morning, look it is already dawn."

Reaching over, Miguel slowly closed the old man's eyes. Picking up the gunny sack he removed a small shovel then began digging the old man's grave.

Standing over the now lifeless body, the boy placed it into the grave. He then, picked up the shovel and began covering it with rich dark brown soil. Miguel made the sign of the cross and began praying. "Lord, please welcome the soul and spirit of your dear servant, Don Demetrus Arturo, a kindly gentleman into your heavenly kingdom. He was a good man who lived on your green earth. In this life, he was the Diviner of San Geronimo, the one who helped your children find life giving water. Now, I lay him down to rest at the base of this great willow tree. It is here that his earthly remains will become part of the reddish brown soil just as the others before him. Then, when the sun sets, his body will become part of the tree of life... Amen"

-- 4 --

"Trooooough...Trouooooogh..."The train whistle echoed loudly as hot white columns of steam rose out of the engine boiler. The sound was high pitched. This sound was mixing with clouds of white steam. The steam continued mixing with bright yellow updrafts of cold early morning air. The conductor was ''Alfredo de Atincio,'' a man of medium height with short black hair and dark black eyes. He had a long drooping brown colored mustache that gave him the look of a thin lonely bloodhound that had not had a good meal in a fortnight of days. He wore a large black conductor's cap that was too large for his small pointed head. On the front of the cap the word "conductor" was written in gold block letters. He also wore a light gray colored vest with a white shirt and dark trousers. Alfredo was now running crazily about the train trying in vain to get all the non-ticketed passengers off.

"Everyone that does not have a ticket must get off!" he shouted, his soft voice barely audible as the passengers were so loud that he could not be heard. The people on the train that day were from many different walks of life, but were all there for the same reason. They were there to see their sons, husbands, and boyfriends off to war. The war had not started yet, but like all wars was inevitable.

There were pretty young girls with anxious looks on their faces who had been praying unceasingly hoping to keep their boyfriends home. And mothers with looks of despair flowing across their eyes like dark reddish storm clouds floating across a darkened desert night. Then there were the proud papa's who knew only too well the misery that war brought on. Yet, there was not one of them present that would not have taken the place of their sons. A lot of the young men who were filling the train lied about their ages because they did not want to be left behind if war did come. They all wanted to serve with their friends, compadres, and the New Mexico 200th Coast Guard Artillery was the best place for that.

"Miguel, will you write to me often?" the pretty young girl with the dark green dancing eyes asked the young solider. They were walking hand in hand toward the waiting train.

"Certainly I will Maria...are you not my wife?"

"Si" Yes, for the last fourteen hours and twenty minutes," she smiled, her beautifully evenly spaced white teeth, lighting up her pretty round face as she looked at him dressed up in his army uniform. The creases of his shirt were freshly starched. His Jump Boots wcrc highly polished and glowed so much that the bright orange rays of the sun reflected off them. It gave her such a feeling of pride that it sent goose bumps rippling up and down her arms.

If the war did come everyone knew that it would not last very long. She loved Miguel so much and now that she was Mrs. Miguel de Otero she felt that somehow her life was now becoming complete. It was at the annual Fourth Of July Celebration in the Las Vegas town square that they met.

Even with the rumors of war spreading throughout Northern New Mexico, like so many wild fires, it caused the boys of Northern New Mexico, including Miguel, to go off and join the 200th Coast Guard Artillery. These were young men who had grown up together and if war did come then they would go off and fight together.

Maria thought about the day she met Miguel as if it were yesterday. It had been a beautiful summer day with the bright purple sun shining brightly sending it's lavender rays of light filtering through the light blue sky. It was at the Fourth of July Celebration in the Las Vegas town square. Jose Martin, along with his group of mariachis, had just started playing ''Ceilito Lindo,'' (one of her favorite waltzes,) when suddenly this handsome young solider walked over and asked her to dance. Of course, she said, "Yes," and he danced divinely, it was love at first sight after that.

"So what are you thinking off my love?" Miguel asked, as they neared the platform where soldiers were still boarding the train. The high school band had started playing "God Bless America" with most of the people stopping what they were doing and joining in.

A large lump filled Maria's throat as she held tightly to Miguel's hand as they both started singing, "God bless America land that I love. Stand beside her and guide her, through the night with the light from above. From the mountains, to the prairies, to the oceans, white with foam. God bless America, my home sweet home... God bless America, my home sweet home."

When they had stopped, Miguel reached down, kissing Maria deeply, holding her tightly as he felt her slipping from his arms. "What are you thinking about?"

"Oh I don't know, mi amor. How long you will be away from me and how much I love you," she wept.

"I also love you so much," he cried, the emotions in his voice reaching her very soul. There were many thoughts flashing through his mind as he held on to her... When would they be back? No one knew for certain... Where were they going...? (That too remained a mystery). Was there actually going to be a war...? No one knew for certain especially after President Roosevelt's speech last night declaring that no American Boys would be sent to die on European soil. But if not Europe, then where?

"I was thinking about what the President said last night on the radio," She whispered, "He said that no boys were going to fight in a war in Europe."

"Si...Yes, but if not in Europe, then where? Some say the Pacific somewhere but no one is exactly sure. Colonel Bertram,our commander, said he didn't think it would be the pacific because the British have such a strong presence there. But if that is true, then why are we trying to arm ourselves so fast?

"I don't know mi Amor, my love. Please hold me I'm so scared!" Maria wept as she clung tightly to Miguel. She felt that she would not be seeing him for a long while.

"Please! Do not worry. I'm sure that I will not be gone that long," he whispered, trying to sound reassuring, but feeling the emptiness that his words made as he boarded the train. Standing at the window seat, he held onto Maria's hand as passengers got off the train.

The train whistle sounded loudly as Alfredo waved his lantern at the engineer from the back of the train. Slowly, the engineer released the brake and the great steam engine started moving forward amid large mists of hot white steam. The well- wishers, feeling the train's sudden movement, quickly gave one another a final hug or quick kiss or strong handshake as wives and girlfriends held tightly to husbands or boyfriends.

"Goodbye...Goodbye"...they all cried out as the great train inched slowly forward with most of the people hanging on to the last moment, then getting off. Miguel was holding Maria, his body halfway out the window holding her in his arms one last time. Lifting her off the ground, he kissed her softly then let her slide gently to the soft grass below as the momentum of the train caused him to loosen his grip.

"Adios Miguel, I love you," Maria cried out, her voice gently floating across the bright orange sunshine. Her voice could barely be heard as the great train picked up speed. The only sound that could be heard was the grinding of metal on metal that the train's wheels were making as they ran along the steel tracks. The train was silhouetted against a broad expanse of steep purple mountain peaks and high dark brown sandstone colored plateaus.

The powerful steam engine hurtled forward carrying the men of the 200th to a far off distant land, a place where the smell of death would fill the air with most of them never returning.

Somewhere in another part of the world, monumental decisions were being made that would soon plunge the world into a war that would cause such mass destruction and death, that the entire planet would never fully recover from.

The Men of the 200th

To the Men from The New Mexico 200th and 515th Coast Guard Artillery who fought and died
Defending the Phillipines later enduring The Death March where many more suffered and Died.
To my Uncle Napoleon T. Sanchez who lost his life serving with the 515th.

What bravery displayed by the men who fought and
Died to turn the tide of history...Where the 200th
From a cold early spring morn to a bright fiery orange sunrise
That is born...Are the 200th
As time grew dark they stared into the night soon would
Come the fight...The men of the 200th
When the battle lines were formed and the enemy drew near
They fought in spite of fear...Were the 200th
Where fire and explosion shook the ground you held
With out a sound...Those of the 200th
When the cannon fire fell...You stared into the gates of hell...
Fought the Men of the 200th
When the battle lines were drawn and death was in the air
You fought without fear...The 200th
For the freedom that you fought for the precious
Time you brought...The men of the 200th
So fast had come the night as they prayed and stood to fight
The men of the 200th
When the lines of history are written
All shall come to know of the bravery that day
As they fought along the way
The men of the 200th

Tsgt Tony Sanchez

General Makato sat at his desk on the small island of Belie near the straights of Formosa. He was the general the Japanese War Council chose to attack the Philippines and defeat the American and Filipino forces. He was a tall man with a neatly trimmed black mustache and dark brown eyes. He had gone to America on a military exchange program having spent two years at Stanford before being suddenly recalled back to Japan. He had liked the Americans thinking they were hard workers knowing they would be a very formidable enemy.

He was known to his subordinates as the general who could saw a man in half with one cold stare. His office was sparse at best. There was the small desk where he was seated at with a picture of Surin, his wife, facing him with a larger picture of the emperor on the wall. There were telephones covered by piles of imperial orders from the general staff that he hadn't even bothered looking at.

At the moment, he was rubbing his stomach which was causing him great distress. He had acquired a mild form of dysentery since landing on Formosa. The medicine that the doctor had given him was of little or no use. Suddenly, there was a knock at the door. Looking up, he ordered the three officers standing there to come in.

"Come in gentleman and be seated," he muttered, a pained expression coming to his face as he nodded to Colonel Tamanjo and Captains Reuko and Hamadee. "I will be with you shortly, after I finish signing these requisition orders."

After bowing, the three officers sat in chairs neatly placed in front of the general's desk. "As you know gentleman, the invasion of the Philippines will began some eight hours after Admiral Nagumos carrier force has destroyed the American fleet at Pearl Harbor. Our assault ships are being loaded even now as we speak. We will land our forces just north of Manila, then drive south to capture it. Our latest intelligence reports tell us to expect about 130,000 American and Filipino troops. Most of them will be Filipinos who are poorly trained, with the rest being American who are poorly supplied. The weapons they have are World One surplus with little ammunition. Most of the aircraft will be destroyed in the initial attack so our resistance should be light but please, make no mistake the Americans though poorly supplied will make a tough fight of it. It will not be easy. Are there any questions?" he asked, looking around at the officers.

"Yes Captain Reuko,"

"There is no doubt that this operation will lead to a great victory and many Americans and Filipinos will be captured. How will they be treated? Will they be accorded their rights under the Geneva Convention?"

"As you are aware, Japan has never signed or agreed to the so called Geneva Convention on how prisoners of war are to be treated. But it is expected that all prisoners are to be treated with our traditions and standards through the benevolence of our great Emperor. Gentleman, soon we will be at war with the greatest military power on earth. This war will be a struggle to the death with no quarter given. Let that be your answer," General Makato said, standing up leaving the room with each officer left with little or no doubt as to what that meant.

A cold rain was falling as the three officers left the meeting. "What do you think will happen?" Colonel Tamanjo asked Captain Reuko.

"I'm sure that the Americans will put up a stiff resistance. They are poorly supplied and we will prevail. After that, if the war lasts long, then I do not think it will go well for us," he said, walking back to his headquarters

As the men of the 200th Coast Guard Artillery settled into their lives in the Philippines, they became home sick with each passing day, uncertain of what their futures held in store. Miguel, along with some of the others was assigned to Clark Field, with life on the whole not being so bad. While at the same time, Colonel Bertram was making sure that his men had plenty to do. There were organized softball games every afternoon and with the Colonel being a stickler for education, made sure that all his men could read and write and were working to get their high school educations. To Miguel, life was pleasant enough but like most men of the 200th he was anxious to get back to the purple mountains of Northern New Mexico.

It was another hot afternoon with Miguel writing some letters back home when Gilbert Ortega, an old friend from Las Vegas, stopped by.

"Hey, Miguel, I and a couple of the guys are going to Manila. They say that the women there look like the girls back home. Personally amigo, I don't believe it, but there is only one way to find out," Gilbert said, looking into a hand held mirror, slicking his hair back, and then placing the mirror in his back pocket.

"I don't think so Gilbert, I have got a lot of letters to write." "Miguel all you do is write letters. We have been here one nth and you haven't stepped outside the base yet. You need to get outside and see some of the country."

"There is a lot going on back home or have you forgotten? As you know, I'm The Diviner for the village of San Geronimo and I must know how this year's crops are doing, especially if there is not enough water."

"Well, you don't have to worry. Yesterday I received a letter from my mother and she said that they were having one of the wettest springs that anyone could remember."

"I'm glad to hear that. It means they will be having a wet spring and a good growing season," Miguel said, getting back to his letter.

"Si...that is correct. Now come on!" Gilbert said, grabbing Miguel by the arm pulling him up."

"All Right...All right but only for a little while, I have other letters to write."

"Sure, why not amigo," Gilbert said, leading Miguel out of the barracks and into the bright fiery red hot tropical sunlight.

Some three miles away from the base at the officer's compound, General Douglas MacArthur was having a leisurely lunch with General Johnathan Wainwright, his deputy commander.

"Well John, what do you think of all these fake war messages that the Japs have been flooding our G2 Section with?"

"It's hard to say Doug, but lately, they have been sending fake messages all over the Pacific. I'm pretty sure that there main purpose is to try and hide their intentions."

"Well, I tend to agree," General MacArthur said between bits of roast beef. "I've been trying to warn Washington for the last six months what the Japs were up to. All I get are reassurances of immediate help being on the way. It's all bull! I sent a message to the president direct, telling him the same thing. Don't think Marshall liked that very much, but do you think I give a damn about that? Were about to get into a real shooting war and many of our boys are going to lose their lives. As you know, the Japs never did sign the Geneva Convention on the treatment of war prisoners

I told the President that I don't need more empty promises. "So what was his response?"

"Well sir, about two days later I got a message from a Mr. Jed Thomas undersecretary of something or other... it's hard to keep track of them all. He went on to say that the president read my message and was going to take it under advisement with a Mr. Frank Knox, Secretary Of The Navy. Now what in heaven's name does the Secretary Of The Navy know about the army, is what I want to know?"

"As you well know Doug, sometimes Washington is a little hard to figure out," General Wainwright said sipping on his cold beer.

"Now listen Johnathan, you are aware, as I am, that all that promised aid that Washington keeps spouting off about is just so much malarkey. We both know that Roosevelt agrees with Churchill that when we do get into this war, the strategy will be to defeat Hitler first. Now, I can't blame Roosevelt for that, I probably would have made the same decision myself," he said taking out his pipe and filling it.

"But, that still doesn't absolve our illustrious leader for abandoning us to the enemy," he said, striking a match getting his pipe going. "We have little food, not much drinking water, no ammunition or supplies to speak of, not to mention very little in the way of medical supplies. I don't know what else you could call it. I know that technically we are not at war yet, but believe me the war drums are beating. It won't take long before were up to our necks in bullets and blood. I only hope that it's the Japs blood and not our very own."

"I know exactly what you mean Doug," General Wainwright said between sips of ice water. "Yesterday, I went on an inspection tour of the newly assigned unit from New Mexico, the 200th Coast Guard Artillery, I believed their called. I will say one thing about them, their fighting spirit and moral are high, but they are poorly supplied. They're low on ammunition with three working artillery pieces with enough ammo for five days at best."

"Well, you haven't heard the worst yet John. Two days ago, I got a message from Admiral Turner. He said that they were escorting a supply convoy that was meant for us, but at the last moment its sailing orders were changed and it was sent to resupply the Brits in Singapore instead. When Admiral Turner questioned about the change, he was told that it came from the highest authority."

"I don't believe it Doug! You mean that a whole convoy was headed our way with everything we need to defend ourselves in this Malaria infested place and it was turned around and sent to Singapore. Just what in God's name are those people in Washington thinking about?"

"Well, one thing is for sure it's not us," General MacArthur said, ordering another scotch and soda, "There's lots more and none of it bodes well for us, if you know what I mean."

"I'm not sure that I want to hear more," General Wainwright muttered, starting to eat the veal he had ordered.

"I can't say as I blame you, John. Frankly, I think Roosevelt and the war department have pretty much sold us down the river. No reinforcements or supplies are headed our way, at least not anytime soon. All we have are empty promises that help is on the way. I tell you, it's a damn shame too. What with the men on half rations now," MacArthur said, (stopping long enough to relight his pipe.) "The effects are already starting to show. Malaria cases are already up by thirty percent and were running out of medical supplies."

Well, from what I hear Doug, the Japs are not big on taking prisoners, it might not be a bad idea for us to fight to the last man. The only problem is that we need something to fight with."

"Yes, and I don't plan on surrendering my command now or anytime soon. The best time to plan for war is before the war starts. I know these men will fight and I plan to lead them to victory no matter what the cost. I know what Roosevelt and that bunch think of me, well, I don't give a damn! If and when The Japs do invade, they will be in for one heck of a fight! I can promise you that! And I swear that to all those mothers and fathers back home. And if their superior numbers with unlimited supplies do push us back then I plan to turn us all into guerrillas, at least what's left of us and fight to the bitter end."

"Doug, if we're going to do that we need to do it soon. Most of the men are getting weaker all the time. With them being already on half rations and with medicines running short, the active cases of Malaria are starting to build."

"Your right about that John, I was thinking much the same thing myself. The time to act is now. I just wish Washington would remember us," General MacArthur said, looking out the large picture window as the dark purple sun was just setting, sending out bright lavender streamers mixed with orange streamers across the dark blue waters of Mantino Bay. General MacArthur poured himself another scotch just as the Filipino band began playing "Sentimental Journey."

Emperor Hirohito was a quiet shy man whose love and knowledge of Biology earned him great respect throughout the world of academia. Having written three books, all of them well received, he was sitting in the study of the Royal Palace. At the time he was having lunch with his wife, Nagako. The emperor was a small thin man with dark brown eyes and a pencil thin mustache.

"So what will happen your grace, will there be a war with America?" Nagako asked, taking an orange, peeling it, then handing it to the emperor.

"Yes, I'm afraid so my lady, the divine wind certainly seems moving in that direction. I spoke with my new Prime Minister "Hideki Tojo", a brutish man certainly not someone I would have preferred, he being a very common person, but in times of war orange blossoms and spiny thorns make strange bedfellows".

"Your Majesty, I have not met him, but have heard many unkind things about his manner."

"That is true, (the emperor said between bits of orange,) "He said that due to the belligerence of the Americans in not allowing us to secure the natural resources we need, then war with them is inevitable."

"Your majesty, could we possible win such a war?" Nagako asked, her eyes wide with wonder.

"Of this, I am not sure and I don't think anyone else is either. I have spoken to Admiral Yamamoto. He told me that if Japan strikes first directly at the American fleet at Pearl Harbor, the attack should cause enough damage to keep America at bay for at least one year."

"But will that be enough? Your Majesty knows, as well as I do, that America is a great power that only needs to be tested to bring her greatness to bear."

"Yes, but Admiral Yamamoto thinks that if the entire American Fleet can be destroyed then President Roosevelt will have to sue for peace, he will have no choice."

"I'm just a women and your loyal and trusting wife, your majesty, but I think striking at America would be a big mistake."

"I'm not so sure that you are wrong, my wife, but the strong winds of war are stirring and like it or not that seems to be the path that we are taking," he said standing up to leave. As he walked away, all the servants that were in attendance fell to their knees in humble adoration.

In the great hall of the Divine Palace, the secretary of protocol was fluttering around nervously as Prime Minster Tojo was addressing his fellow ministers. "The time to strike is now! Everything will begin on December 7th," he screamed, slamming his huge fist on the podium his words echoing throughout.

But what of our latest cable received from Kurosan, our Ambassador to America, saying that President Roosevelt was asking for direct negotiations with the emperor? "Sukate Tanaska", the minister of the navy, asked.

"I have already spoken with his majesty with all the rest being just a formality. When it comes to matters of state security, the cabinet will decide what is best for Japan! The future of this country rests with its armed forces."

"With Germany winning great battles in Europe I don't think the war will last long. If we don't strike at America now, then due to our lack of natural resources, Japan will become nothing more than a second class power. Gentleman! That is something I refuse to let happen! Admiral Yamamoto is here and he will go over our plan of attack."

Walking into the room, Admiral Yamamotto bowed to the members of the general staff, then walked briskly to the lector's podium. Admiral Isoroku Yamamotto was short and squat in stature. His head was shaved leaving his dark piercing eyes staring into the souls of his audience. He had been wounded in the Russian-Japanese war. He later attended the Naval War College. In 1912 he studied at Harvard, later becoming naval attache' in Washington.

"My fellow countrymen, as you know war with America is coming. The plans are already set for attacking the American Fleet at Pearl Harbor. We will use a total of six aircraft carriers with over one hundred eighty planes. All six carriers will be used in the initial attack. There will also be twenty six support vessels. Everything from battleships to light cruisers to destroyers. Nothing will be spared. We will also have a separate group of submarines to sink any American ships that escape our initial attack.

Moving to a large map, he continued, "The fleet will sail from Tankan Bay in the Kruel Islands, departing in strictest secrecy in route for Hawaiian waters. This will all take place on the 26th of November. We will cross the Northern Pacific avoiding all normal shipping channels. The fleet will be 200 miles from Pearl Harbor on the 7th of December. At 0700 hrs we will began the attack. Torpedo Planes, Dive Bombers, and Horizontal Bombers will began the attack. We will also use four squadrons of fighter planes for air cover and escort. At approximately 10:00 hrs a second wave of aircraft will be launched insuring total destruction of the American fleet. Make no mistake about it, America is a great country with vast natural resources, so once the war starts it will be to the death with no quarter given," he said walking quickly off the stage and out the great hall Just south of Honolulu, Captain Natusho Mahre had strict orders to dock the giant passenger ship "Mako" in Honolulu Harbor and take on all people of Japanese descent who wanted to go back to Japan. With war clouds brewing the Japanese Government made sure that all her citizens were given the opportunity to go back home if they desired to.

But to Lieutenant Akio Kaede, fighter pilot off the carrier Suyro, (he would be the one to lead the fighter cover for the attack on Pearl Harbor) was on board for other reasons. He'd taken up a disguise as a ships steward with complete access to the ship. As he moved about the ship he was studying and making notes on how the tides were effecting the passenger ship as it passed through the straits near Pearl Harbor. He was also keeping track of the deep currents and wind conditions that the Imperial Navy ships would face in launching their attack on Pearl Harbor.

Captain Mahre was to alter his course when necessary, making sure to enter Hawaiian waters through the northern route between the Aleutians and Midway Island, then turn directly south to Hawaii. This was exactly the same route that Admiral Nagumo's carrier task force would take to strike Pearl Harbor.

The mission was well planned just like everything pertaining to Pearl Harbor, leaving nothing left to chance. In another part of the world some five thousand miles away, President Roosevelt was meeting with his Cabinet.

The president seemed nervous and somewhat irritated as he placed a cigarette in the holder, striking a match, then lighting it. He inhaled deeply allowing the smoke to drift aimlessly up into the room. All the members of his staff were there, including General Marshall along with his staff.

"Gentleman, I think the time is getting near when Imperial Japan will strike. They have been building up their war production at a faster pace than ever. Our latest magic intercept made that very clear. As you know, it is the wish of this administration that Japan should strike the first blow. From the reports that we have been receiving, that is going to happen sooner than any of us think."

"But Mr. President, if what your saying is true, don't you think that General MacArthur should be rushed reinforcements and supplies immediately," Frank Knox Secretary of the Navy asked?"

"Yes, I quite agree with you Mr. Knox. The only problem is that all the supplies that we can spare have already been put at General MacArthur s disposal, is that not correct General Marshall?"

"Mr. President, I assure you that everything that could be spared has been sent. That unit that arrived two weeks ago, the 200th Coast Guard Artillery from New Mexico, is already in place and operational. I think General MacArthur will be in good shape provided they are not taken by surprise."

"I agree the element of surprise would be the enemy's greatest weapon. We must make sure that all our forces are made well aware of that," President Roosevelt said, thinking about all the momentous decisions that lay ahead of him, wondering if he would be up for the job.

"I assure you, sir, that General Short and Admiral Kimmel have been made aware of this fact. In fact just two days ago the entire Island of Hawaii came off full alert. General Short reports that the men were somewhat tired of alerts, but first indications are that all emergency procedures seem to be functioning well," General Marshall said.

"Well, General, I'm glad to hear that, but it is imperative that we keep our guard up at all times," President Roosevelt said, tipping his cigarette holder, acknowledging the men that he had chosen to lead these United States through the darkest hours it would ever face.

Johnny Yamitze,was an unassuming young man, who worked at the Japanese Consulate for the last two years. He was tall and extremely well built with deep dark set eyes and a wide smile that showed off a set of perfectly matched teeth. He had dark wavy hair, always keeping himself in perfect shape. He was an expert in Judo giving free lessons at the Japanese American Friendship Club (off Hamilika Drive in downtown Honolulu.) It was rumored that he came from a wealthy family and that his job at the consulate had been arranged by his father. Johnny was well thought of, making friends easily, seemingly being found of naval personal who he often befriended, treating them to lavish meals at expensive posh down town restaurants.

Johnny Yamitze, was Captain Kendo Fujemate of Section X of the Imperial Navy. Section X had been set up by Admiral Yamamotto to gather all possible information on the American Fleet docked at Pearl Harbor. They answered to Yamamotto personally and were given the highest priority.

Johnny Yamitze had been doing the same thing, going over the same route ever since arriving in Honolulu one year before. He always set his alarm for five o'clock, took a quick shower, and then put on his running shorts and shoes. He ran the same route down Hauula Drive for one mile then crossed over the docks down ocean drive, then on to Pearl Harbor Park. Everything looked the same as it had two days ago, with most of the fleet tucked in nice and neat like so many dominoes waiting to fall. Picking up speed, he ran further down the harbor looking for the American Aircraft Carriers, (the main targets.)

They were not in sight .That was disappointing news at best and something that Admiral Yamamotto must be made aware of. Running closer to the harbor entrance, he could see the marine guards as they stood watch. Jogging past their guard shack, he waved at them running up the small hill that lay just ahead. Moving to the top of the hill, he looked down to the center of the harbor where the Air Craft Carriers should have been docked. "They must have gotten under way last night," he said, running further south, turning back on Hauula Drive to where he lived.

Ensign David Fields was from Waco Texas, and had been in the navy for the last two years. He was tall and lanky, (in a West Texas sort of way) and like his father had fiery red hair and clear blue eyes. Two years ago, the furthest thing in young Davids mind was signing up for a four hitch in the United States Navy, but that all changed when one Naval Captain Fred McClure showed up on his doorstep.

He had just graduated from Sam Houston State Teachers College, with not a care in the world on his young mind on that fateful day. Both of his parents had been Southern Methodist Missionaries assigned to Okinawa where he was born. He spent the next the next seventeen years of his life growing up with the Okinawan people, learning their customs and speaking their language. He had also been taught to speak and write formal Japanese fluently, often going to main land Japan with his parents on missionary trips. He could still remember Naval Commander Robert McClure's words after he had spoken to him for the first time.

"Listen David," he went on to say, "Your country needs you. There are very few Americans that can read and write Japanese like you do." It had been one of those long hot West Texas days, the kind that seem to go on forever. To David, Commander McClure appeared short for a naval officer, he had coal black hair with light green eyes.

"Well, I'm not sure that I want to go into the Navy. I don't think fighting a war is exactly in line with my religious beliefs," he said, looking Commander McClure directly in the eye.

"I realize that, besides you're going into Naval Intelligence. You'll be assigned at Pearl Harbor and be commissioned an Ensign in The United States Navy, what could be better than that?"

"Nothing, but don't I have to go to officers school first?" "Don't worry about that, you'll be taking ROTC Classes at Pearl. David, I'm not going to bullshit you. This job is so important that Admiral King personally signed your orders and in the Navy it doesn't get much higher than that. Naval Intelligence did a complete search of the whole country for the qualifications that we were looking for with only two other candidates showing up. One was a young asthmatic living in Spokane, Washington, the other, a thirty year old engineer in Belleview Maryland, who has since turned up missing."

"OK Commander, you sold me. Besides, I always did want to live in Hawaii."

"Good...Good...I know that you're going to enjoy it," Commander McClure smiled, slapping him on the back, then walking away, leaving him to contemplate his new life as an Ensign in The United States Navy.

David received his orders two weeks later and was assigned to the 14th District of Naval Intelligence Honolulu. He got a room at the Officers Billets at Pearl Harbor, where he made himself as comfortable as he could. He would be working with the local FBI Office and Army Intelligence. His job consisted of reading coded enemy intercepts and helping to keep track of suspected enemy agents.

Every afternoon, Commander Barrett, whose job it was to keep everything at 14th District Naval Intelligence running smoothly held a meeting with his G-1 agents of which Ensign David Fields was its newest member.

"So what do you think of this fellow Yamitze," he asked, as he passed a photograph around.

"I don't think much of him," (2nd lieutenant Sarah Clark of Army G2 section) said." Sarah was a Yale graduate class of "38". She was a tall brunette with light green eyes and a somewhat too friendly smile to match. "We had a tail on him since he got here with nothing much to show for it. He's got plenty of spending money."

"Yeah, the little twerp has got that, "Captain John Avery said. He was what would be considered a lifer in the Marines, having already served seventeen years. He was of medium height, with dark brown eyes and short cropped light blond hair. He had the look of an infantryman, someone that knew his business. "As far as we can tell his father is a wealthy business man in Tokyo, making sure that junior has plenty of folding money. I wish my old man had done that with me," he said, chomping down on the half smoked stogie he griped between his teeth.

"I think your right Captain Avery, but in this business you never know," Commander Barrett said. "So what's your take on him, Fields?"

"I can't say for sure, sir, having lived among the Japanese for so long, I have come to learn that sometimes the important things are not what matter most. The inconsequential is what bears watching. I would like your permission to keep an eye on Mr. Yamitze."

Alright David, Yamitze is yours. As you all know, negotiations with Japan are not going well. Most of the folks in Washington think the Japs are stalling. So with not much time left, I'm afraid we must find out just what they are up to. Now, this comes from a pay grade a lot higher than mine, so let's get on it...leave no stone unturned and spare no expense," he said as the meeting broke up.

"So David, you really think that Yamitze is the key?" Sarah asked, as the others left the building.

"It's hard to say if he's the key. I do think he knows a lot. Just what that is, I'm going to find out.," David said, walking out the door and into the bright Hawaiian sunshine.

"So tell me David, what's up with this guy?" She asked, hurrying out the door.

"I don't know, but sometimes that's just as important as what you do know."

"Well, I think there is something going on. I have a feeling that we'll be going to war," Sarah said.

"I think your right about that, how about lunch on me?," David smiled.

"That would be fine," she said as they walked into About two miles north of where Johnny Yamitze lived, Ensign David Fields awoke earlier than usual. The alarm had been set for five- thirty but the luminous dials staring back at him read five o'clock. Scratching his head, he knew that Johnny Yamitze would be taking his run off Hauula Drive and he wanted to follow him. Quickly getting up he put on his running shorts, laced up his shoes, picked up his hat and water bottle and walked out the door. He had been following Johnny for the last three days with his pattern always seeming to be the same. He knew that Johnny's run would be winding down, but that was ok, because he wanted to run the exact route he had just finished.

Walking down the stairs, he started running down Hauula Drive where Johnny had just finished running. David ran up to Pearl Harbor Park, then past the main entrance where the marine guards were posted. Running further down, well passed the marine guards, he had a good view of battleship row and he couldn't help but think what good targets they would make for Japanese bomber and torpedo pilots. "Damn!" he thought, "They're sitting ducks the way there parked and lined up." Moving further on, he looked to where the Air Craft Carriers were usually anchored. He remembered Commander Barrette saying that they would be getting under way late last night. "Wait a minute! If we know that, then who else knows it!" he said to himself, running as fast as he could to the nearest phone.

Running up the steps to the enlisted man's quarters, he grabbed the phone out of the young sailor's hand who was on CQ duty, pushing the receiver down he called Commander Barretts private number. "Hello Commander Barrett, it's David, listen I just got through following Johnny Yamitze on his early morning run. They know where all the battleships are parked along with all the support ships. They also know that our carriers are not in port. I have strong reason to believe that they are going to attack us and damn soon too. That is why I have to pick up Johnny Yamitze. He is the only one that can confirm that." Honolulu Grill, which was right across the street.

"Well David, I was just going to get a hold of you. I've got some big news for you. It's about one Johnny Yamitze. We ran an inqiry about him to include his photo through our FBI and also British Intelligence and guess what our Brit friends came up with? It seems like he had been assigned as a Japanese observer from the Imperial Japanese Navy. His real name is "Captain Kendo Fujemante" of Japanese Naval Intelligence. I'm not so sure we should pick him up yet. If we do then the Japs will know were on to them." "I realize that Commander Barrett, but this is imperative. I believe the Japs are going to attack and soon. I'm talking all-out war and I mean right here at Pearl...Soon commander...soon."

"Ok David, you've convinced me. I'll sign the arrest warrant, but wait for help and don't try and take him alone... David! David!" Commander Barretts voice trailed off into an empty receiver as the sailor who had been on CQ picked up the phone placing it back on the desk. Looking out the window, he could see Ensign David Fields running crazily down Huluki Drive trying to get to Pearl Harbor as fast as he could.

David felt that he had to move fast he knew that he didn't have much time. Call it instinct or call it luck, but he did know that Japan was going to attack Pearl Harbor and he had to do all within his power to stop it.

Meanwhile, Admiral Yamamotto from the battleship Actum had just flashed the message to Admiral Nagumo on the carrier Akagi..."Commence the attack...Commence the attack...six aircraft carriers The Akagi..The Hiryu...The Kaga...The Shokaku...The Sorya...The Zuikaku...all turned into the wind launching their aircraft into the light early morning orange sky. It was a total of one hundred eighty three aircraft led by Commander Fuchida, all turned west headed for Pearl Harbor.

Where would Fujemante be? David thought, as he ran out of the CQ Office. "Where would he be at?" he asked himself, "Think David, since he helped map the attack, where would he be watching from? It had to be someplace where he could relay damage assessment...Damn! That's it!" he shouted, as he took off running toward Ford Island. The small knoll directly to the east would make a perfect observation point and battle assessment platform. As he reached the knoll he could see where someone had built up a small wall of sand bags.

"Hello Johnny Yamitze...or should I say Captain Kendo Fujemante," David said, walking toward him.

"You know who I am, yet I have not had the pleasure," Fujemante said, looking toward David a thin smile crossing his dry pinkish lips.

"You don't need to know who I am. All that you need to know is that I'm placing you under arrest," David said walking toward Fujemante.

"Brave words coming from an unarmed man," Fujemante said, wondering how long it would take him to remove this intruder.

"It's like I said, you're under arrest. You can come peacefully or under force, but either way you're coming in." David reached out for him only to find himself flat on his back as Fujemante garbed his arm throwing him over his shoulder.

"It's obvious to me, that you don't know who you're dealing with young man and under different circumstances, I would let you live and be about your young life, But! These are not normal times and I'm afraid I'm going to have to kill you," Fujemante said, grabbing David, tossing him to the ground bringing his elbow into David's stomach causing the air to be driven out of him.

Standing up to defend himself, David managed to get air back into his lungs, moving cautiously, he measured Fujemante as he circled around him as a wolf would circle his prey looking for a weak spot. "This is almost too easy," Fujemante said moving in for the kill.

Suddenly, out of the east there came the loud sound of Nagumos Aircraft as they began making their bombing and strafing runs. The sudden sound of the aircraft caused Fajemante to look up and that was all that David needed as he swung a powerful roundhouse kick smashing into the face of Fajemante, causing him to fall backward stunned by the power and quickness of the kick. He lay in the sand as Japanese Zeros began peeling off attacking the American Ships that lay spread out before them. For some reason, Fajemante stood up and began running toward the strafing Zeros waving his arms wildly overhead. Jumping for the sandbags, David covered his head as he saw Fajemante running toward an incoming Zero. Watching the Zero as it headed to where Fajemante was running, it cut loose with its thirty caliber machine guns, tearing Captain Kendo Fujemante to pieces.

"Damn!" David cried out, as he stood up watching the carnage that was taking place on Pearl Harbor. There was smoke and fire everywhere bombs were exploding. The sounds of the wounded and cries of the dying filled the air. Wave after wave of Japanese fighters and dive bombers kept coming, dealing death and destruction totally unopposed

The President awoke an hour earlier than usual. He did not seem to be sleeping as much as he usually did. "It's been a long time since you've slept through the whole night Franklin," he whispered, rubbing his legs trying in vain to bring some life back into them. There was a soft knock at the door as Albert Long, his personal assistant stood outside his bedroom door.

"Yes Albert, do please come in," he said sitting up in his bed as Marvin Milton, his valet, was fluffing up his pillows then pouring him a cup of tea. "Thank you Marvin, I swear you take better care of me then even my own mother did.

"Thank you Mr. President, I appreciate that" he smiled as he walked away. Looking up, The President noticed that Commander Richard Block, his Naval Attaché, was standing at his door with a very worried look on his face.

"Richard, do come in and from the look on your face I can tell that the news is not good."

"Sir, I want you to understand that these reports are all preliminary, but it looks like the Japanese are going to strike at us, we just don't know where"

"You know Richard, we will just keep watching their Naval Fleet and the last report I had was that they were all in their home ports," The President said, reaching for the pack of Chesterfields, taking one out and lighting it.

"Yes, I know sir I wrote these reports but somehow they left out the back door and now were not sure where they are."

"I can only imagine," the president said, rolling his eyes, pressing his pager as his valet walked in. "Marvin! Let's hurry and get me dressed, this country is going to war and soon I suspect."

"Yes Sir, Mr. President," his valet said, helping him to the bathroom.

President Roosevelt was having a late lunch with Harry Hopkins in the upstairs study.

"Well Harry, what do you make of it? We have lost an entire Japanese Fleet, our navy has no idea where there at, they say they snuck out the back door. Well, the pacific is one hell of a big back door."

"Excuse me, Mr. President," Grace Tull, his personal Secretary interrupted, "It's Mr. Frank Knox, Secretary of the Navy and he says it urgent."

"Yes, Mr. Knox, this is your President, go on please..." the look on the presidents face changed quickly as he listened to the phone. " You're sure about this Mr. Knox? OK thank you," the president said, placing the receiver back.

"What is it Mr. President?" Harry Hopkins asked.

"Well, you know Harry, about the Japanese Fleet that no one seems to know where their at, well, we know where there at now, they're attacking Pearl Harbor! Even as we now speak!"

"Good God! Mr. President, you can't be serious!" "I'm afraid so Harry, I'm as we thought they would be..." FDR said, staring off into space. "Harry, I've got a speech to write. In the meantime, get the Cabinet together. I want to meet with them tonight, right here in The White House."

"Yes Mr. President," Harry Hopkins said hurrying out of the room to a small private office where he began calling members of the cabinet.

It was around five pm when President Roosevelt called Grace Tully to his study. "Sit down Grace. I'm going to dictate a speech, it's not long," he said, lighting a cigarette, then began talking..."Today, December Seventh, 1941- a date that will live in infamy. The United States of America was suddenly and deliberately attacked by naval air forces of the Empire of Japan. The United States was at peace with that nation and at the solicitation of Japan,was still in conversation with its government and its emperor, looking toward the maintenance of peace in the Pacific. Indeed, one hour after Japanese air squadrons had commenced bombing the American Island of Oahu, the Japanese ambassador to the United States and his colleague delivered to our Secretary of State, a formal replay to a recent American message. And while this replay states that it seemed useless to continue the existing diplomatic negotiations, it contained no threat of war or of an armed attack. It will be recorded that the distance of Hawaii from Japan makes it obvious that the attack was deliberately planned many days or even weeks ago. During the intervening time, the Japanese government has deliberately sought to deceive the United States by false statements and expressions of hope for continued peace.

The attack yesterday of the Hawaiian Islands has caused severe damage to American naval and military forces. I regret to tell you that many American lives have been lost. Last night the Japanese forces also attacked the Philippine Islands...As commander in chief of the Army and Navy, I have directed that all afraid so."

"But how can that be Mr. President? The Emperor says he wants peace!"

"Well, I guess The Emperor's wishes were not as important measures be taken for our defense. But always will our nation remember the character of the onslaught against us. No matter how long it may take to overcome this premeditated invasion, the American people in their righteous might will win through to absolute victory."

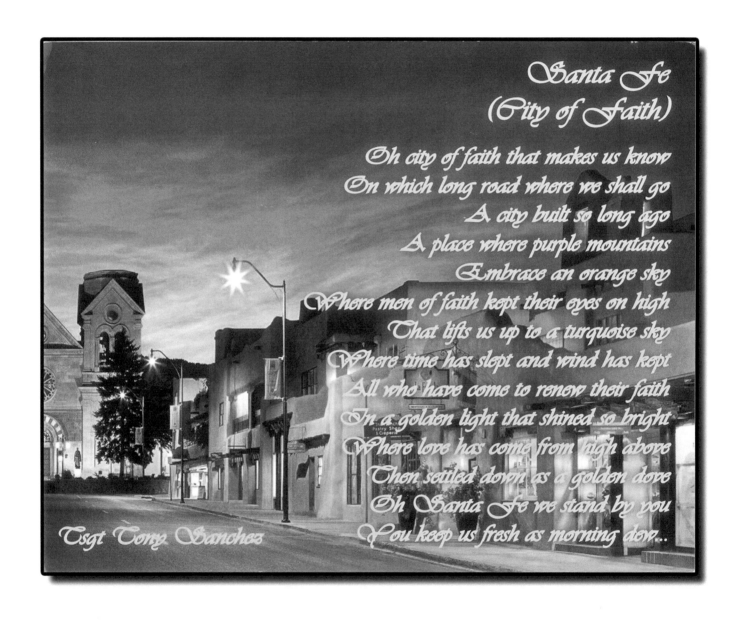

Santa Fe
(City of Faith)

Oh city of faith that makes us know
On which long road where we shall go
A city built so long ago
A place where purple mountains
Embrace an orange sky
Where men of faith kept their eyes on high
That lifts us up to a turquoise sky
Where time has slept and wind has kept
All who have come to renew their faith
In a golden light that shined so bright
Where love has come from high above
Then settled down as a golden dove
Oh Santa Fe we stand by you
You keep us fresh as morning dew...

Tsgt Tony Sanchez

Miguel de Otero was a wise man who knew many things. He lived in the village of San Geronimo in the Sangre de Cristo Mountains of Northern New Mexico. He was a strange old man or so many of the villagers thought. To his family and friends he was Miguel de Otero, a good and honest man. To others he was "el Viejo" (the old one). To the younger ones he was "el loco" (the crazy one). Yet he did not mind being called "el viejo" because he was old. Or even "el loco" since maybe he was a little bit crazy. However, to the people that needed him most when their wells went dry and their crops wilted in the fields from the hot dry turquoise sun, he was the Diviner, the one who could find water.

The village of San Geronimo was located at over eight thousand feet. It was at this great height and higher that the old man heard of people becoming ill due to altitude sickness. He was happy that he had never suffered such a thing. However, he was not sure what altitude sickness was. He knew that if this altitude sickness had befallen him, then surly he would have known. Perhaps he caught it and never knew. Miguel had heard of such things happening to people. He could have dreamt he had it but never did. "Am I not a strong old man?" he asked. "So surly if I had gotten this altitude sickness, I would have known. "Una cosa muy mala," "surely a bad thing to have," he whispered, deciding not to think about it.

The old man was tall and thin, carrying himself well, though past the age of eighty seven. His skin was dark brown like dry chestnuts, wrinkled and leathery, with the small dry white blotches of skin cancer now showing on the back of his neck. They were the result of all the years of working in the hot, dry purple sun, of Northern New Mexico. His hands were large with many rough calluses and many scars. Yet, his eyes were clear and young and strong, the same color as the light powdery blue sky overhead.

The shack that Miguel lived in had inside plumbing and little else. It was made from pine logs that he and some friends cut

so long ago. It had one large room with a cast iron stove sitting in the middle of it. This is where he cooked his meals. There was also a table with two chairs and a sink to wash in. Off to the side were two bedrooms, one where he slept, the other used for storage.

As the old man slept that night, he dreamt that he was back in the army before the war came. He joined the New Mexico Coast Guard Artillery at age 16. Like most of the other boys from New Mexico they were a tough bunch of young men, who later on made strong disciplined soldiers. He liked to remember the good times like the bivouacs, sleeping out under the stars in the mountains of Northern New Mexico. Of the friendships, and the sure joy of breathing fresh mountain air and drinking the clear water from fast rushing mountain streams. He never liked to think about December 7th when the Japanese struck Pearl Harbor and then invaded the Philippines. He survived the Bataan Death March but many of his friends had not. That was the hard part, knowing that he had lived while so many were killed by the brutal hands of the Japanese.

When Miguel was a young man, he never prayed or thought about God. Then the war came and all the men of the 200th learned to pray. It was after the fall of Bataan and during the Death March, that prayer was the only thing that any of them possessed that the enemy could not take away from them. It was these moments of talking to God that made it possible to survive the sheer brutality that was cast upon them. No matter how hard the enemy tried, their spirits were never defeated.

He often thought of Gilbert Ortega, his best friend, who was killed by the Japanese as they moved forward to take Clark Field. He and Gilbert shared a bunker together when they struck. There was enemy fire coming from all around. They were picking off Japs up and down the flight line when Colonel Bertram ordered them to retreat. When they started falling back, Gilbert was shot in the chest. Miguel picked him up and began carrying him back across the fight line to where the rest of the men were retreating to.

"Don't die Gilbert! ...Please don't die!," he remembered crying, holding Gilbert's lifeless body in his arms.

"You must go on Miguel," Gilbert whispered, pushing his arm away from him. "You must live to tell the story of what happened here. Of how the boys from New Mexico fought bravely and died for their country, even in retreat we died like men..." "Hang on Gilbert ...Please don't die!" he wept.

"Miguel, you are The Diviner for San Geronimo. You must make it back so you can find water when there is drought and little hope. You give life giving water to those people who love you," were the last words Gilbert spoke.

Miguel remembered as he and some of the others from the 200th started digging Gilbert's Grave. Reaching over he took his dog tags, then began praying, "Lord, welcome my friend Gilbert Ortega to you and all your heavenly places. He was a good friend and one I now leave to your love and care," after having said the prayer, Orlando and the others joined in the retreat to Corregidor.

Moving from the bed, Miguel got dressed. Walking to the wash basin, he filled it with water from a pitcher nearby. Washing his face and hands, he dried himself with a nearby towel. Setting the towel down, he moved over to the wood box, took some wood chips out placing them in the stove. He then struck a match and began fanning the embers getting the fire going. The old man knew that the boy would be coming soon and would be hungry. Taking some larger pieces of wood he placed them in the stove, feeding the embers, giving them life.

"I will make breakfast for Roberto because he will be hungry as most boys are," the old man said. Reaching for the icebox, he took out some bacon and three eggs. Taking a frying pan, he cleaned it off with a nearby rag. Miguel could not remember the exact time he had started talking to himself. He felt that it must have been sometime after Maria died. "Edes muy Viejo, you are an old man,pero muy fuerte, but still strong," he smiled laying strips of bacon across the bottom of the pan. He then filled the coffee pot with water.

Looking out the window Miguel saw that it was still dark. He knew that it was getting lighter as he began to feel the warmth of the fiery purple sun. It was starting to rise in the east, pushing back the dark grayish night time clouds. The sun was warming the earth with bursts of light lavender energy, moving to the frying pan he turned the bacon over, cracked the eggs with one swift motion of his hand, frying them on the side. Instinctively, he turned his head toward the door. There was a soft knock. Looking up,the door opened with the boy looking in.

Standing in the purplish light of the early morning sun, the boy's slim build reminded him of a baseball pitcher that he had seen on television. This player pitched for the Dodgers of Los Angeles. His name was Enrico Paize...or was it Pedro Ortiz? The old man was not sure. His memory was now clouded with the dimming light that old age brought on. "Miguel, how can you forget the name of such a great player as this?" he asked, looking toward the boy.

Roberto was tall and thin for his fifteen years. His hair was light brown with clear hazel eyes. Then there was that bright smile that seemed to light up his face whenever he asked Miguel a question. The young boy loved the old man because he taught him so much about life.

"Roberto! Please come in and sit down, I am making breakfast for you."

"Thank you, Don Otero. It is good of you to feed me," the boy said, wiping his feet before entering. He used the word "Don" when addressing Miguel because it showed the great respect that he had for the old man.

"Sientate' por favor, please sit down." I am making breakfast for you."

"Thank you Don Otero," he said, as he quickly started eating "Esperate' un momento, wait a moment please. Are we not supposed to give thanks to God for the food he has provided for us?" "Yes, you are right sir," the boy said," I forgot and I am sorry."

"That is all right my son. You are a growing boy, but we must not forget the Lord and all the good things that he brings into our lives. I will say grace for the both of us," Miguel said as he bowed his head bringing his hands together in prayer. "Thank you Lord, for this good food. Please bless this day, as we go out into a dark and sinful world. It is something we gladly do to bring your love and Light. Amen.

"You prayed very well," the boy said as he went back to eating.

"I will join you," Miguel smiled, refilling his coffee cup, then sitting down.

Watching the boy eat the old man thought of many things. Mostly he reflected on his own mortality and just how much the boy had to learn. There was not much time if the boy was to take his place. Roberto would be the next Diviner for San Geronimo. Future generations would look to him for life giving water. "Roberto, es muy vivo, he is very wise for one so young," he whispered, as his thoughts went to other important matters.

Now he was thinking about baseball and the time he traveled to the small town of Las Vegas, just south of Taos. Roberto was living with his Aunt Josefe'ta at the time. He was pitching for Robertson High School. The boy was fourteen then with long skinny arms and legs. He pitched well striking out many players.

"I was remembering last spring and the great game you pitched against Saint Michales. I never saw you play better," the old man said, his eyes resting on the boy.

"Gracias Don Otero, I felt good then. Coach Aragon said that if I continued improving I might receive a scholarship at some large university. I'm not sure that I would like that."

"Por que, Why not?"

"Because I would not know anyone there and would be unsure of myself."

"You must not worry my son," the old man said, "someday you will grow up and be a man, and then you will have great confidence."

"I hope so, Don Otero. Right now I'm just a boy with many things to learn."

"Si, and you are showing great improvement," the old man spoke as that faraway look came into his eyes when he began thinking about the past. "I remember when I came back from the war, I would travel to Albuquerque to watch the Dukes play in the old stadium at Tingley Beach. They had good baseball teams back then but I have lost track of them."

"That was a long time ago," Roberto said. "They are no longer called The Dukes, but are now called "The Isotopes". There is a new stadium but I don't know where it is, "he said, as he finished eating. Gathering the dishes, he placed them in the sink, where he washed and dried them.

"Is that not a strange name for a baseball team, The Isotopes, what does it mean?" "I'm not sure and I don't think anyone does either." "That is very odd," the old man reflected, as he thought about baseball and the great love he felt for it "Is it not strange to name a baseball team something that no one knows the meaning of?"

"Yes, I agree with you Don Otero. The world seems strange sometimes," the boy said, thinking of his future and where it would lead him. The old man was teaching him the art of divining for water and the boy loved him for that.

Looking around the shack, the boy could see that the old man needed many things. "I must get him some new towels to dry his hands with, the ones that he is using are old and faded, also boots for his feet," (his were old and worn with a small hole on the side.) He saw where the old man was stuffing newspapers in his boot to keep the cold out. "How could you be so inconsiderate and not think of his needs," the boy thought as he put away the dishes.

"So tell me Roberto, what do the villagers say about me?" he asked, taking some papers and tobacco from a nearby coffee can. Listening to the boy, he rolled a cigarette. He then struck a match. Sitting back in the chair, he watched the light blue smoke as it slowly drifted into the air.

"Some say that you are a great war hero, that you suffered greatly," Roberto said, placing the dish towel back as he sat down.

"Si...Si...Yes...Yes...please go on."

They say that it happened right after the Philippines fell to Los Japones...The Japanese. I do not know much about this. When we studied about World War ll in school...I was sick missing three days."

"I remember it, but you are back in school and that is where you must stay. The world is kinder to those who have education," the old man said, thinking back to the Philippines and how beautiful it was before the war came. There would always be a special place in his heart for the Filipinos. They were a kind and honorable, reminding him of the people of Northern New Mexico.

"Tell me about the Death March, Don Otero, was it bad? I do remember hearing about it. I think you must have suffered greatly. When I was working at Ortega's Grocery Store there was always a large picture of Gilbert, their son. Mrs. Ortega would always cry whenever she talked about him."

The old Man looked at the boy, his eyes filling with tears. "Gilbert was my best friend and he died in my arms. We buried him there at Clark Field. After being liberated from the POW Camp I brought his dog tags back to New Mexico and gave them to Mrs. Ortega. I will always remember him and all the other brave men who gave their lives holding the Japanese army at bay with little more than our bare hands, giving our country time to prepare for war. It is always a sad mistake not to be ready for what the future holds in store for you. As a country, we made that mistake. I hope we never do again."

"Was there death and suffering all around? Do you have hatred in your heart for those who did such bad things to you?"

"Yes! The smell of death was everywhere, with many brave men dying. No, I do not feel hatred. To hate is a bad thing and

there should never be any room for it," the old man said, smoking the last of the cigarette."

"I think you and the others were very brave. I do not think I could ever be that brave."

"We were not brave, we just did what we had to do."

For many years the old man suffered. It would often happen when he thought about the war. It was after a pilgrimage to the holy shrine of "El Santuario de Chimayo" that he was able to forgive. He tried not to dream about the war but still the dreams came, but not as often as before. Now he dreamt of the beauty and elegance of Northern New Mexico, the golden yellow sunrises along with the fiery orange and purple sunsets. It was a place that he loved. It filled his soul with peace and joy.

"Come, we must go now, there is work to do," Miguel said, picking up the gunnysack that he had resting against the table. Taking a bottle of water, he placed it inside. Leading the boy to the back door, they walked into the early morning light. The bright warm sun was starting to rise over the soft peaks of the Sangre de Cristo Mountains. The delicate rays of light were starting to warm the earth as the old man and boy walked down the dirt road that led to the village.

"Here, you must carry the willow branch," the old man said, opening the gunnysack, removing a large perfectly formed willow branch. "I cut it from a willow tree high in the Sangre de Cristo," he said handing it to the boy.

"Thank you," the boy said holding the willow branch as they neared the house of Margarita Martinez.

Walking to the front door, the old man knocked softly. Soon an elderly women answered. She was small in stature with dark brown almond eyes and graying hair. Her face was round. She was wearing a faded blue housecoat. Her eyes were sad as if she had been crying.

"Hola, Hello, Don Otero, how good it is to see you." "Hola, Margarita...it is good to see you. I understand the well drillers were not able to find water."

"Si... that is true and it cost me a lot of money. I have nothing to show for it!"

"Who did the drilling?" the old man asked.

"It was Max Baca of "Baca Water and Drilling". When I told him how displeased I was at all the empty holes he had dug, he laughed. I said, "Max, look at all the empty holes you have dug in my back yard. There is nothing to show for it! Where is the water that you promised me?" He just smiled as he spoke to me.

"Senora Martinez! I did not promise you anything," he laughed.

Max was a short barrel chested man with crooked teeth and a bad disposition. He shaved his head and had a dark scar running down the side of his cheek. It was rumored that he had received it from a rival gang member while serving time in prison. He was the reported leader of a local motorcycle gang "Los Perros Negros". "I cannot help it if you bought land where no water exists."

"But you said nothing of this before,"

"Look this is the contract you signed. Do you see your signature?" he asked pointing to where I had signed.

"Yes, but I was confused."

"Confused or not, it says right here that there is no guarantee that water will be found. Lo siento muncho, I feel for you, but I am a businessman not a miracle worker. I cannot find water where there is none."

"You're a ladron!...Thief!...and I thank God that your dear sweet mother, may she rest in peace...is not here to see what the love of money has done to you."

"Senora, please leave my mother out of this. She has been dead these last ten years that has nothing to do with how I run my business. I am sorry, have a good day."

"Yes, you have changed Max and all for the worst, I'm afraid. I should have called Miguel de Otero, The Diviner of San Geronimo. He would have found water and at a cheaper price."

"Miguel de Otero! You mean that crazy old man, don't you? The one who walks around with a stick in his hand claiming to have found water. He's loco...Crazy! He can find nothing," Max said to me as he left."

"And now Don Otero, I have nothing to show for all the money I've wasted! " she started crying lifting up her hands in despair the tears rolling softly down her face.

"Do not worry Margarita, I will find water for you. My fee is two hundred dollars. You may pay me when you are able and I do suggest that you find another well drilling company. I have heard many bad things about Max de Baca and his company."

"Gracias...Thank you Miguel. I do not know what I would do if it was not for you. After Max left, I called my son Philippe. He is a doctor in Albuquerque. He too said negative things about you."

"What did he say?"

"He said that what you did was just superstition. He called it "hocus-pocus" and that I should not waste my money. But I already did, Max got two thousand dollars from me and I have nothing to show for it."

"You must not cry," the old man said placing his hand on her shoulder. "I remember Philippe. He was a smart boy and as I recall a good "beisbolista" tambien. So now, he is a doctor, an honorable profession. He can help people when they are sick.

"He is a good son who got a baseball scholarship at the University of New Mexico. It was because of this that he was able to become a doctor."

"Your son has done well. This is Roberto my apprentice," Miguel said, pointing to the boy. "We will go to the back of your house. We will find water."

"I know that you will Miguel because I have great faith in you and your young helper. I should have called you in the first place."

"That is all right Margarita," the old man said as he and the boy walked to the back of the house. "What do you know of Max de Baca?" the boy asked. "Only that his family has been running De Baca Water for the last fifty years. They charge much but find little water. After his father Federico died, Max started going down the wrong road. "Una semilla mal, a bad seed. It seems like he spends more time in prison then out."

"Do you think that there is any water in the back yard of Senora Martinez's?" the boy asked, as he felt the warm golden sunshine on the back of his neck. He felt excited as he always did whenever he and the old man looked for water.

"I don't know," Miguel said scratching his head. "It seems that all Max was after was some easy money. Now we will find out," he said, leading the boy to the back of the house.

"Look at all the holes that have been dug!" the old man said, pointing at the freshly dug holes with piles of dark brown sand around them.

"There are many," Roberto said.

"Yes, and none of these are deep enough to find water." "So they took her money for nothing."

"I'm afraid so, but do not worry, we will find water. Watch and learn, for soon you will be doing this," the old man said, taking the willow branch out of the boys hand.

Lifting up the branch, the old man offered it to the four winds. Walking slowly, he prayed..."Oh Lord, I pray that there be water here...I also pray for Roberto my young helper for I know that I will be joining you soon. Strengthen him and protect him...in Jesus Holy Name...Amen."

The old man's voice reminded the boy of the wind as it whispered for all to hear. As it moved across the vast brown and purple desert speaking of where it had been and where it was going to go. Holding the willow branch tightly across his body, the old man's movements were slow and precise. The steps he chose were measured and rhythmical, much like Diego d la Sol, the great Spanish Flamenco Dancer of Northern Santa Fe. In the soft lavender light of the early morning sky, the willow branch changed into the partner of life of Miguel de Otero. Suddenly, it was lifted high into the sky. It then came crashing down as the force of newly found water drove it into the dark rich soil.

"There is the place, mark it well," the old man said. "I see it!" the boy cried out.Taking some stakes and a small mallet from the gunnysack, he ran to the place where the old man was standing, grabbing one of the stakes he drove it into the dark rich soil.

Looking up, the boy kept his eyes on the old man. His steps were slow and graceful as he held tightly to the willow branch. It was as if the old man were clinging to life itself and could not let go. Then he could hear the old man singing the words that were of long ago. They told of the beginning of time when God created the universe... "Let there be light," he sang, and there was.

Holding tightly to the willow branch the old man spoke softly. "Now is your time Roberto," he said, loosening his grip, passing the willow branch on to the boy, then falling to the ground. "It is not supposed to happen like this, but with death, it comes at its own calling." Miguel coughed as his life drained from his face. "Roberto, you are a man now and you must carry me up to the "Sangre de Cristos" to where I showed you. I must be laid to rest under the tree of life."

"Don Otero, you cannot die and leave me now. I have much to learn," the boy wept, holding the old man's head in his lap. "You must not die," he kept repeating while others from the village came out to see.

Margarita began praying the rosary, she then covered the old man's face with a plain white scarf. Then the warm desert wind whispered, "Forever more," lifting the white scarf off the old man's face carrying it high into the light blue sky, then higher into the dark purple sun where it could not be seen.

The boy picked up the willow branch along with the gunnysack, following the villagers as they carried the old man's body into the church. The boy stopped crying, for he was a man now and the new Diviner, for the village of San Geronimo.

The End

Sunflower

Oh beautiful Sunflower
All glittering and new
As bright as sparkling sunshine
So fresh as mountain dew
You speak of golden sunshine
One petal at a time
When the ancients gathered
Across the purple plains below
They brought their people together
Where the turquoise life-giving rivers flow
They danced the dance of life
Their fertility to renew
To welcome Father Earth
Sister Rain
Brother Wind and Mother
Golden Moon
Oh sunflower your beauty
Is divine
It makes us all as one
Throughout the sands of time

Tsgt Tony Sanchez

EPILOGUE

As the boy stood at the base of the great willow tree, the purple sun was just starting to set in the west. The villager, who had helped him carry the old man's body back to the Terento Valley, had left. They had brought

him up to the small ledge, then into the large cavern then placed "The Diviner" next to the tree of life.

The boy signed the ledger just as the old man had told him to, then he proceeded to the great tree where the old man's body rested. Slowly, he dug the grave, then placed the old man's body into it. He then started covering it with rich dark soil. Reaching into the gunny sack he took the measuring stick out, cutting the divining rod from the great willow tree.

He then stood over the old man's grave praying. "Lord, you called forth your son Miguel de Otero into the next life. He was a good man who suffered greatly in war, yet was able to forgive his enemies. May I be able to follow his example in leading the good people of San Geronimo, in their never ending search for life giving water...Amen.

Our Lady

Our Lady Queen of Heaven
Oh eternal rose
A quiet wind a gentle breeze a golden fallen leaf
Gentle woman glorious child
Voice of angels songs of joy
Queen of heaven light eternal
Oh golden morningstar
A red rose of light where stars shine bright
A mothers love a gentle dove
Oh shining from above
A choir of angels a crown of gold
Oh perfect shining star
A song of joy a mothers love
A voice as gentle as a dove
Oh heavenly eternal rose

Tsgt Tony Sanchez

Printed in the United States
By Bookmasters